Nadakkave, Kozhikode, Kerala
Tel:0495–4020666
www.insightpublica.com
e-mail: insightpublica@gmail.com

Who's The Strongest
Valery Suslov
Drawings by *V. Trubkovich*
Tomorrow ? Yesterday?
Boris Zubkov
Illustrated by *I Kabakov*
Insight Publica Facsimile Edition: July 2020

ISBN 978-93-90355-67-9

Those fantastic
Soviet Books Again

"All of us still have those fond memories of the books from the erstwhile Soviet Union, which were once extensively circulated here, in Kerala - books of fabulous tales, riveting scientific facts and enchanting illustrations which stole the readers' hearts. They left in us an indelible impression and an unforgettable reading experience. An experience still ever-green in us, Malayali diaspora.

As the Union got dissolved, those charming books of tales too vanished, turning them into cherished memories of nostalgia. Yet, readers have relentlessly been looking for those inimitable books. That was why we, the INSIGHT PUBLICA, published a few of them in the same mode. We are grateful and glad to say that readers whole-heartedly backed us in realizing the project.

During the execution of our mission, we could fathom the depth and breadth of a great nation's remarkable literary project. Those sublime Soviet stories traversed in translation into many a nation and many a language. Those books were ubiquitous-not as merchandise, but as products of culture.

The fantastic bolstering that INSIGHT PUBLICA could get is the impetus that drove us daringly to undertake the mission of reprinting and republishing those Soviet works in Indian languages.

You readers need not anymore be discontented with the scanned copies of these books. INSIGHT PUBLICA will help reach into your hands those very books with the same freshness and warmth.

Let us present you again those fantastic Soviet Stories with humility and pride."

Sumesh Insight

Content

WHO'S THE STRONGEST

Valery Suslov

Alec was always asking Anton questions.
"How high is the sky?"
"What's deeper, the sea or the ocean?"
"Can you dig a hole in the Earth and come out on the other side?"
Today, too, he was skipping along, trying to keep up with Anton saying, "Who's stronger, an elephant or a whale? And who's the strongest of all?"

Anton was in a hurry. He was grown-up and had many things to do. But Alec kept right on.

"Tell me who's the strongest?"

"See that crane over there?" Anton said. "It's lifting a railway coach. That means it can lift an elephant or a whale as easily as a feather."

This was something Alec had never thought of. He was silent for a few moments and then asked, "But what's stronger than a crane, Anton?"

"See that blue electric locomotive pulling fifty freight cars? All of them are loaded to the very top. That means the locomotive is much stronger than the crane, doesn't it?"

"Yes," Alec replied slowly. "Then what's stronger than an electric locomotive?"

"Look over there," Anton said, picking Alec up and standing him on the embankment railing. "See that ship being loaded? It'll take lumber, bales, barrels and crates far across the sea. Its hold is so big it can take on twenty-five trains. Perhaps even thirty. It will carry them all across the sea."

That was something to think about. Alec even stopped skipping. "Anton, but what's the strongest of them all? T H E V E R Y   S T R O N G E S T?"

"Stop pestering me, Alec. Try to figure it out yourself."

Alec thought and thought but couldn't decide.

"Come on, tell me," he said at last.

"Who makes the crane lift its long boom? Who makes it work?"

"I know! The crane operator!"

"And who makes the electric locomotive move along the rails and pull fifty freight cars?"
"The engineer."

БАТУМИ
BATUMI
HANDLE WITH CARE!

"What do you need to make a ship sail across the sea?"
"I know! A captain and a crew!"

"And who built the crane, the electric locomotive and the ship?"
"PEOPLE."

"WELL, THEN, WHO'S THE
STRONGEST OF ALL?"
"WE ARE."

BORIS ZUBKOV
TOMORROW?.. YESTERDAY?..
ILLUSTRATED BY I. KABAKOV

What Happens Every Day

Early in the morning the sun shows the fiery top of its head over the woods and hills. All day long it sails across the sky, and when it disappears toward evening, it takes with it light and warmth. Long, long ago people became frightened when the sun disappeared at night. "Suppose it's gone for good and will never return!" they would exclaim. But after noticing for many years that day always follows night, they came to understand that the sun is certain to return. Day and night come again and again.

Fishermen on the shores of oceans noticed that every day the ocean came up close to their huts and then moved away. It seemed to have a mighty chest that rose and fell as it breathed. The tide came in and went out over and over again.

In the spring wide rivers become wider. They overflow and bring silt to the fields. When fields are covered with silt, they produce rich crops. People would wait for the rivers to overflow and notice how often this happened.

Day follows night. The ocean tide comes in and goes out. The seasons of the year follow one another in strict order. Nature seems to be counting something. What?

Time!

Summer passes and winter comes again. This is a new winter. It is not the one that left us last year. And Today is not the same as Yesterday. Yesterday... today... tomorrow. Time does not return. Time goes forward, always forward.

A good way to measure Time is to count what is repeated over and over in the world around us.

A thin sickle of a moon grows day by day until it

becomes a silvery full moon. People used to celebrate when a full moon appeared. They reckoned Time in this way too, from celebration to celebration. From one full moon to another made one lunar month. Many peoples reckoned Time by lunar months. In Russian the word "month" is often used for the moon.

Long ago peoples who lived far from each other never saw each other. But everyone knew that if the sun was getting hotter, it was time to plant, and if the days were getting cooler, it was time to harvest the crop and lay in a supply of firewood.

People already knew the seasons of the year. They knew Time. This knowledge brought them together. They lived apart, but Time said to them, "The sun rises for all of you. You all live on one planet."

Time united people.

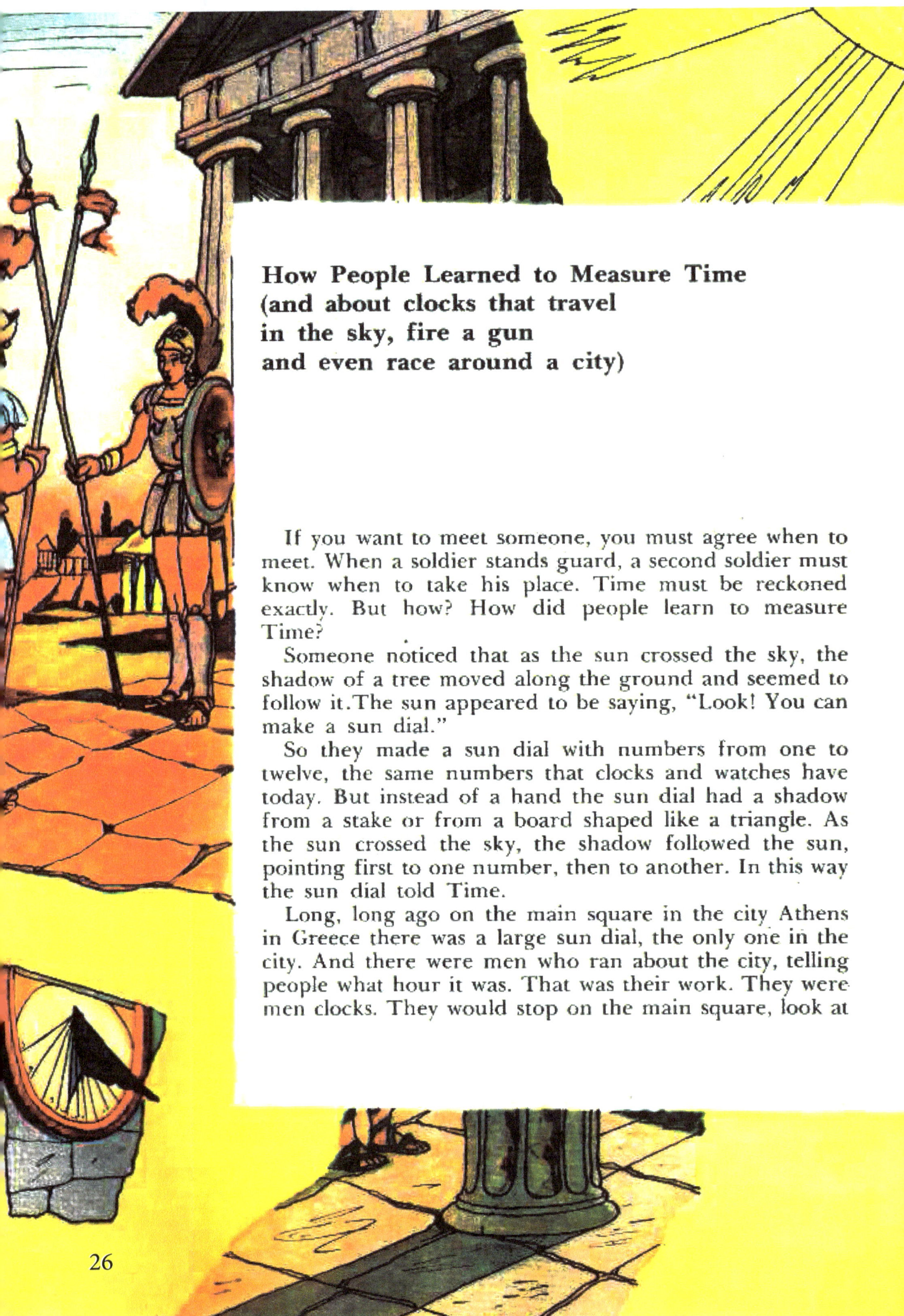

How People Learned to Measure Time
(and about clocks that travel
in the sky, fire a gun
and even race around a city)

If you want to meet someone, you must agree when to meet. When a soldier stands guard, a second soldier must know when to take his place. Time must be reckoned exactly. But how? How did people learn to measure Time?

Someone noticed that as the sun crossed the sky, the shadow of a tree moved along the ground and seemed to follow it. The sun appeared to be saying, "Look! You can make a sun dial."

So they made a sun dial with numbers from one to twelve, the same numbers that clocks and watches have today. But instead of a hand the sun dial had a shadow from a stake or from a board shaped like a triangle. As the sun crossed the sky, the shadow followed the sun, pointing first to one number, then to another. In this way the sun dial told Time.

Long, long ago on the main square in the city Athens in Greece there was a large sun dial, the only one in the city. And there were men who ran about the city, telling people what hour it was. That was their work. They were men clocks. They would stop on the main square, look at

the shadow on the sun dial, and then run about the city, letting everyone know the hour of day. People gave them a little money for this.

That is how a clock raced around a city.

There was a clock, too, that fired a gun. Again it was

the sun that made it fire. A piece of glass shaped like a belly can collect the rays of the sun in a small point that is very hot. People took such a piece and with it directed the sun's rays onto gunpowder so that at twelve noon exactly the rays set fire to the powder.

"Bang!" went the gun. "Twelve o'clock! Do you hear? Twelve o'clock!"

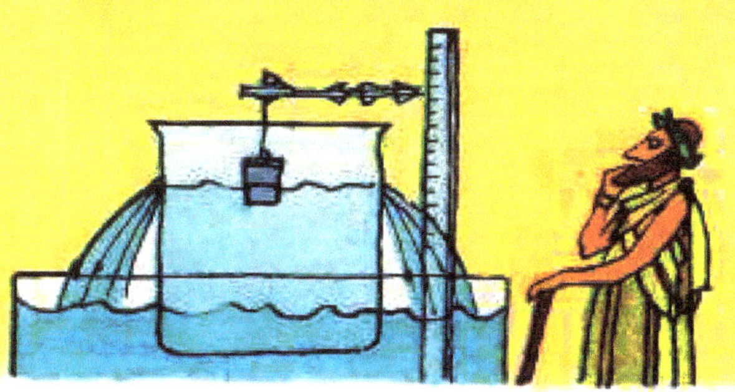

With twelve guns instead of one a whole clock could be made.

The only trouble is that sun dials do not tell Time at night or on days when clouds hide the sun.

Long ago there were water clocks, too. Water dripped from one dish into another. A float moved up and down as the water rose or fell, and on the float was a hand that showed the Time. This clock told the Time at night as well as in the day. But as the water evaporated, more had to be poured in.

Do not imagine that water clocks were always so simple, consisting of only two dishes and a float. Sometimes the water set in motion a complex mechanism. Then a toy knight in armor would pop out of a window or a toy boy would float on the back of a dolphin. Sometimes the water made a ball drop into a metal dish with a tinkle to strike the hour. People even invented a water alarm clock. What a clock it was! It had arms that seized the leg of the person asleep and tried to pull him out of bed.

All these strange mechanisms were driven by the force of falling water.

Finally, people got the idea of using a weight instead of water. The first clocks with weights were made about one thousand years ago. They had only one hand, the hour hand.

Then a spring appeared in clocks to replace the weight. If you take a key and wind up your toy car, you are tightening a spring inside. Now if you put the car on the floor, the spring will begin to unwind, the wheels will turn, and the car will race across the floor. The same thing happens in a clock. The spring makes all the wheels and hands move.

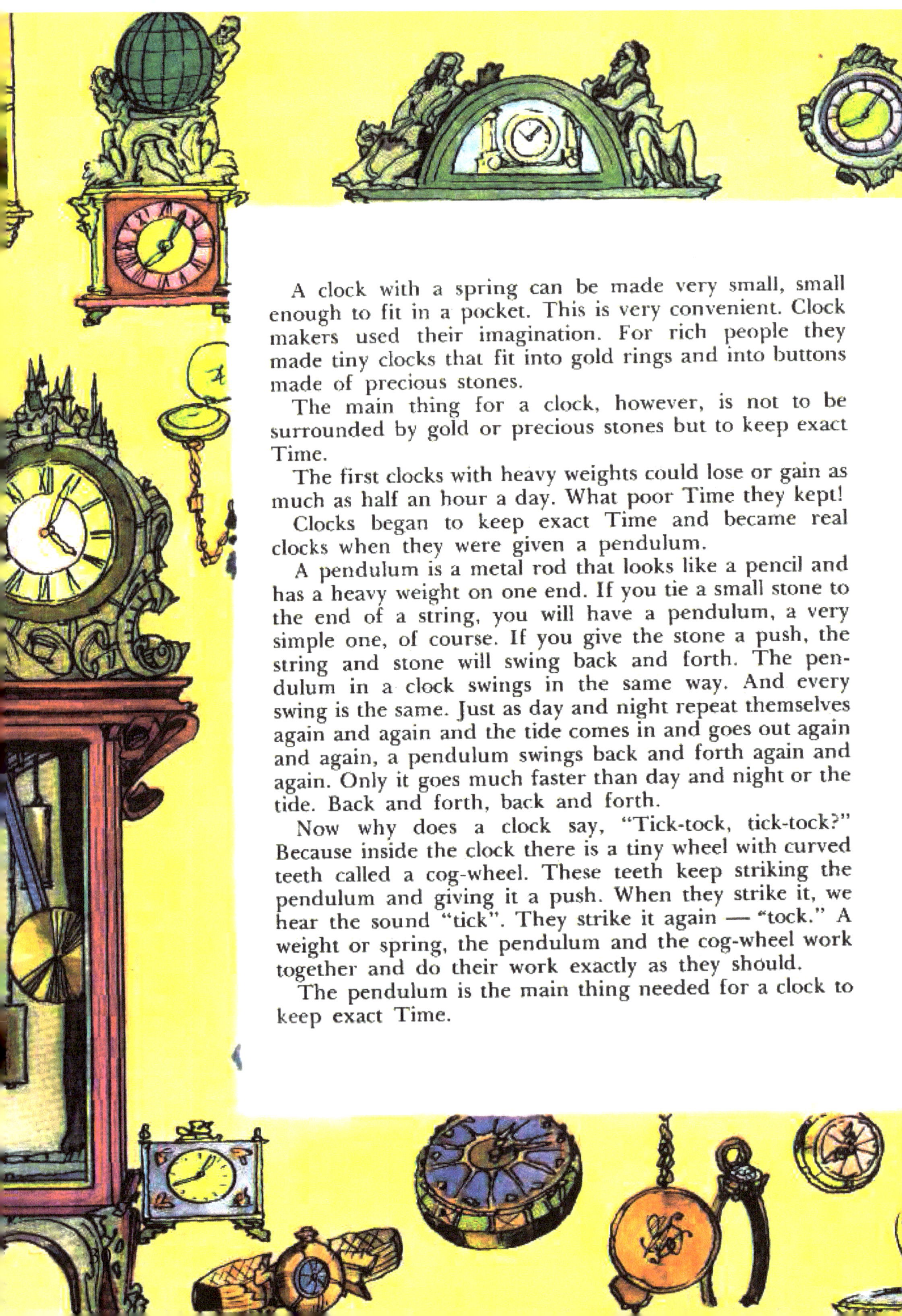

A clock with a spring can be made very small, small enough to fit in a pocket. This is very convenient. Clock makers used their imagination. For rich people they made tiny clocks that fit into gold rings and into buttons made of precious stones.

The main thing for a clock, however, is not to be surrounded by gold or precious stones but to keep exact Time.

The first clocks with heavy weights could lose or gain as much as half an hour a day. What poor Time they kept!

Clocks began to keep exact Time and became real clocks when they were given a pendulum.

A pendulum is a metal rod that looks like a pencil and has a heavy weight on one end. If you tie a small stone to the end of a string, you will have a pendulum, a very simple one, of course. If you give the stone a push, the string and stone will swing back and forth. The pendulum in a clock swings in the same way. And every swing is the same. Just as day and night repeat themselves again and again and the tide comes in and goes out again and again, a pendulum swings back and forth again and again. Only it goes much faster than day and night or the tide. Back and forth, back and forth.

Now why does a clock say, "Tick-tock, tick-tock?" Because inside the clock there is a tiny wheel with curved teeth called a cog-wheel. These teeth keep striking the pendulum and giving it a push. When they strike it, we hear the sound "tick". They strike it again — "tock." A weight or spring, the pendulum and the cog-wheel work together and do their work exactly as they should.

The pendulum is the main thing needed for a clock to keep exact Time.

· CLOCK MECHANISM ·
11 12 1 2 3 4 5 6 7

What is the most exact clock today?

On the wall of a large empty room you can read the words "Standard Time of the Soviet Union." Here in this room electric lights form figures that show the hours, minutes and seconds. Clocks all over the Soviet Union check the Time by this clock because it is the most exact of all. It gains or loses one second in thirty thousand years! Other countries too have their most exact clocks and check them with each other by radio. There is a Worldwide Time Service.

So even today Time says to us, "You all live on one planet."

When the sun rises, a new day begins. The earth turns and as it does, new cities and villages face the sun. So clocks show different times in different cities. When it is noon in Vladivostok, it is only early morning in Moscow. To make it easier to reckon Time, people have divided the world into 24 Time Zones. You can see them on this page. There are 24 because there are 24 hours in the day. When it is two in the afternoon in Vladivostok, it is seven in the morning in Moscow and four in the morning in Paris and London. If you travel from one Time Zone to another, you must set your clock one hour ahead or one hour behind.

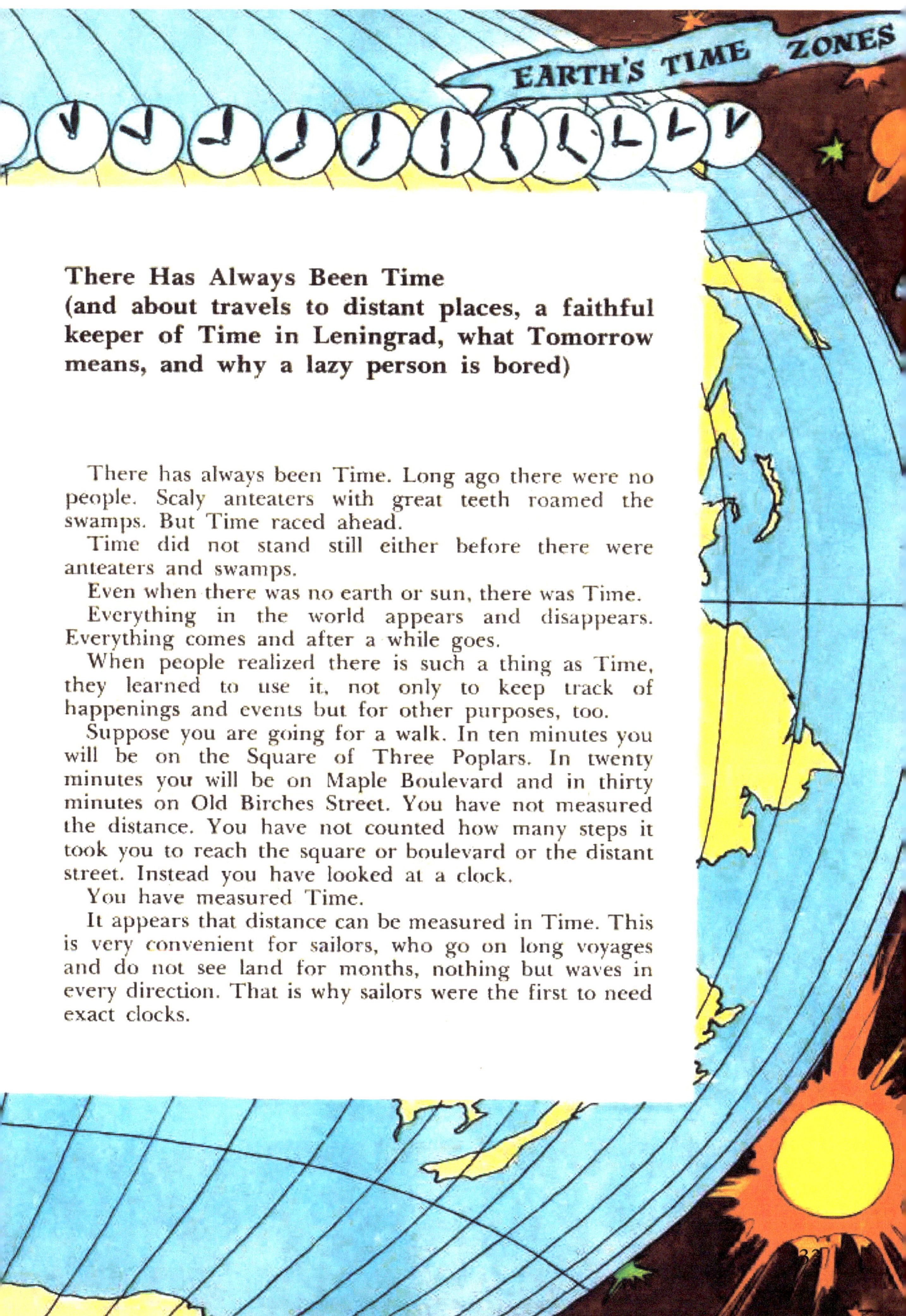

There Has Always Been Time
(and about travels to distant places, a faithful keeper of Time in Leningrad, what Tomorrow means, and why a lazy person is bored)

There has always been Time. Long ago there were no people. Scaly anteaters with great teeth roamed the swamps. But Time raced ahead.

Time did not stand still either before there were anteaters and swamps.

Even when there was no earth or sun, there was Time.

Everything in the world appears and disappears. Everything comes and after a while goes.

When people realized there is such a thing as Time, they learned to use it, not only to keep track of happenings and events but for other purposes, too.

Suppose you are going for a walk. In ten minutes you will be on the Square of Three Poplars. In twenty minutes you will be on Maple Boulevard and in thirty minutes on Old Birches Street. You have not measured the distance. You have not counted how many steps it took you to reach the square or boulevard or the distant street. Instead you have looked at a clock.

You have measured Time.

It appears that distance can be measured in Time. This is very convenient for sailors, who go on long voyages and do not see land for months, nothing but waves in every direction. That is why sailors were the first to need exact clocks.

Icebreakers push their way through ice to the stations of explorers in the Arctic. Ocean-going ships sail to far-off lands. Submarines travel under water. All the captains must have clocks that tell the exact Time.

Wherever people go, they take clocks. They cannot live without them. They must keep track of Time. Sometimes people have performed acts of heroism to keep clocks going.

When German troops were just outside Leningrad during the Second World War, it was bitterly cold, so cold that the hands of the city clocks stopped moving. The clock on the tower of Moskovsky Station stopped and no trains left for Moscow or for anywhere else either.

But there was one clock in Leningrad that went all the 900 days and nights of the siege. This was the clock on Mendeleyev Tower. A legend was told about this clock. It was said that underground the clock was connected by electric wire with Moscow and that the Germans were

looking for the wire in order to cut it, but could not find it.

In fact, this was simply an old clock with a very heavy weight, a weight so heavy that it had to be lifted with a special windlass. An old worker named Ivan Fedotov did this.

The old man was growing weaker all the time. It was hard for him to get to the tower through the snowdrifts. It was still harder to climb to the platform where the windlass stood. And it was almost impossible to lift the heavy, heavy weight with the windlass. But day after day Fedotov mustered all his strength and lifted it. And the hands on the clock on the tower moved and told the Time. The people of Leningrad had so little to be glad about, but at least they had this. They would say, "The clock is alive. Time is moving. Victory is ahead."

Whenever you or I, or any one tells a story, he says, "It happened yesterday" or "This morning I saw", or

"Tomorrow I'm going to do this." When we tell about events in our lives, we always speak of Time. We say "Long ago.... Not so long ago.... Just recently.... Not very soon...." We think constantly of Time. All life long we measure Time.

You remember Time by interesting events, for exam-

ple, you talked with someone who has seen and done a lot of things or you visited a strange city or you read an interesting book.

The more you see, learn and hear, the more you live. Your life is full. If you are lazy and do nothing and do not know how to do anything, you do not live. You simply waste Time. Life is uninteresting if you have nothing to do.

For a lazy person Time stands still.

The Clock Inside Us
(also how oysters and bean plants remember Time, and who night owls and early birds are)

Now let me tell you about an amazing clock. It has no hands, spring or weight. And, most surprising, no one has ever seen it. But everything living on this earth has such a clock. Birds, fish, flowers, cats, trees, and you and I all have this clock.

More than 200 years ago the French astronomer de Mairin gave up studying the moon and planets for a while and instead of counting the stars decided to study bean plants. Just ordinary bean plants. He transplanted them from the garden to a dark cellar, where they saw neither the sun nor the moon. Day is like night in a dark cellar. But the plants went on living just as before. In the daytime their leaves straightened and stood up and at

night they drooped as if they were going to sleep. Those bean plants felt the passage of Time! This was how people first learned that plants have an internal clock.

And now something that happened quite recently. Oysters were caught on the seashore and flown by plane thousands of kilometers to a lake. When they reached the lake, the moon was coming up, but back there by the sea the sun was still shining brightly and the oysters continued to live by their own clocks. They opened their

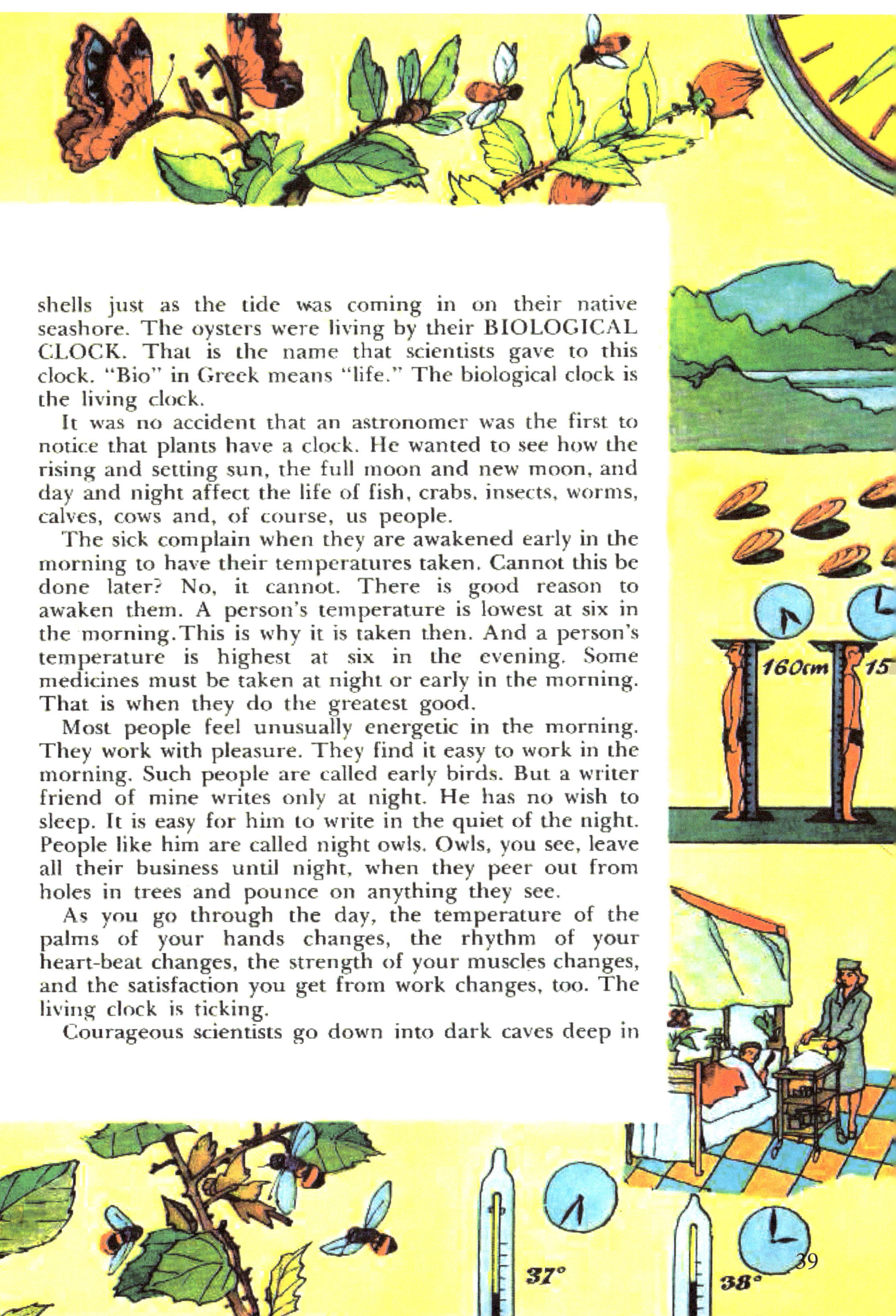

shells just as the tide was coming in on their native seashore. The oysters were living by their BIOLOGICAL CLOCK. That is the name that scientists gave to this clock. "Bio" in Greek means "life." The biological clock is the living clock.

It was no accident that an astronomer was the first to notice that plants have a clock. He wanted to see how the rising and setting sun, the full moon and new moon, and day and night affect the life of fish, crabs, insects, worms, calves, cows and, of course, us people.

The sick complain when they are awakened early in the morning to have their temperatures taken. Cannot this be done later? No, it cannot. There is good reason to awaken them. A person's temperature is lowest at six in the morning. This is why it is taken then. And a person's temperature is highest at six in the evening. Some medicines must be taken at night or early in the morning. That is when they do the greatest good.

Most people feel unusually energetic in the morning. They work with pleasure. They find it easy to work in the morning. Such people are called early birds. But a writer friend of mine writes only at night. He has no wish to sleep. It is easy for him to write in the quiet of the night. People like him are called night owls. Owls, you see, leave all their business until night, when they peer out from holes in trees and pounce on anything they see.

As you go through the day, the temperature of the palms of your hands changes, the rhythm of your heart-beat changes, the strength of your muscles changes, and the satisfaction you get from work changes, too. The living clock is ticking.

Courageous scientists go down into dark caves deep in

CLOCKS OF FLOWERS
chicory
poppy
dand[elion]

the earth to see how their living clocks will behave in such a strange place and such difficult conditions. They live in the caves without seeing either a clock or the sun for weeks and months at a time. It is difficult to live alone in the dark but very interesting. One scientist spent forty days and nights in a cave. He thought he was there only twenty-five because his biological alarm clock lost count of Time. But even in the dark and silence underground it said to him, "Time is passing."

What does a living clock look like? What are its "spring," "hands" and "pendulum?" No one knows. The living clock remains a mystery, but we know for certain that it exists.

Some people can say to themselves in the evening, "I must get up at seven o'clock tomorrow. Not one minute later." And, sure enough, they wake at exactly seven. But a boy whom I know sets two alarm clocks and is late for school anyway! If he reads this story, he will probably be glad and say, "I'm not to blame that I'm late. My living clock runs badly."

However, I think we can learn to wake up when we need to.

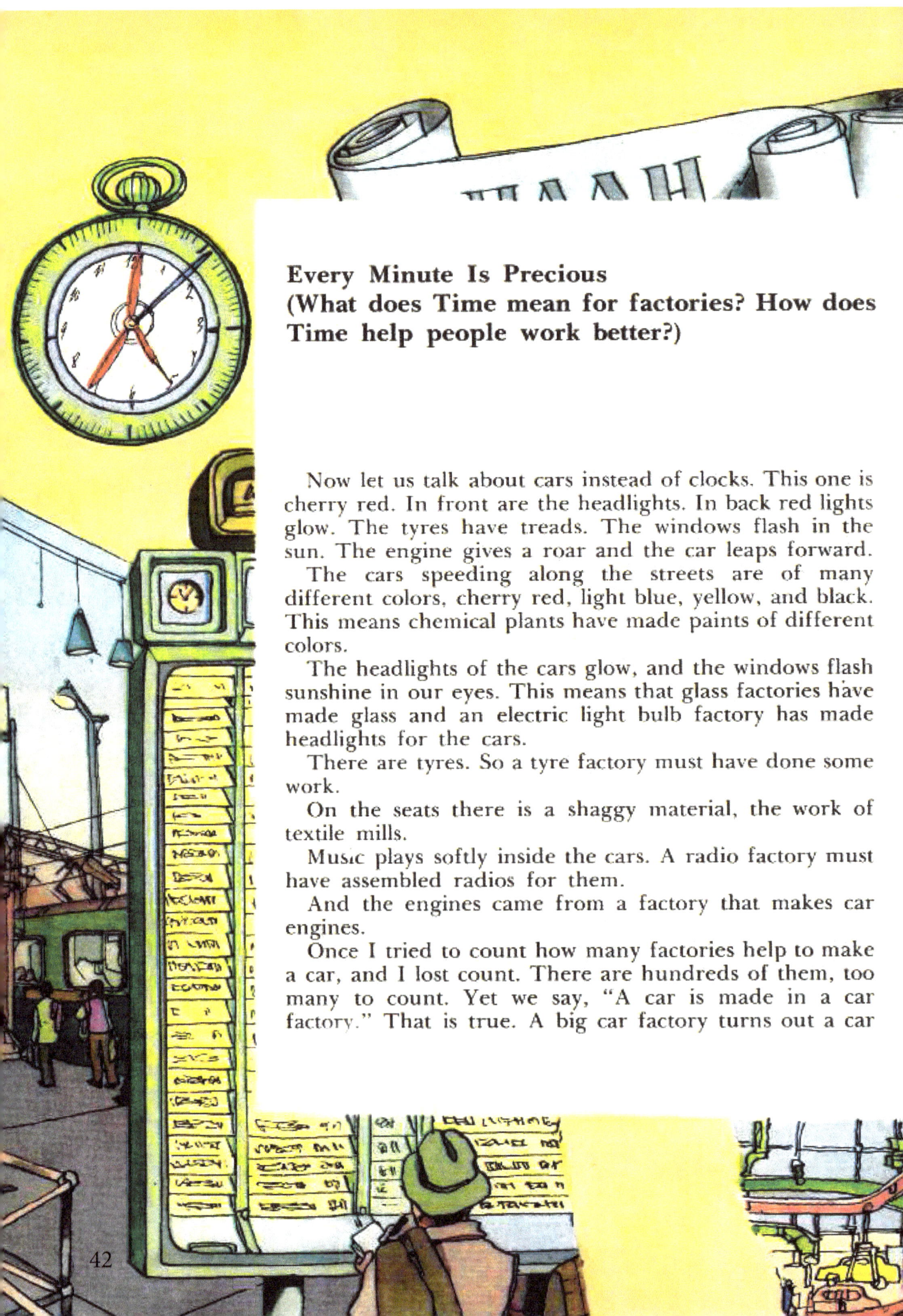

Every Minute Is Precious
(What does Time mean for factories? How does Time help people work better?)

Now let us talk about cars instead of clocks. This one is cherry red. In front are the headlights. In back red lights glow. The tyres have treads. The windows flash in the sun. The engine gives a roar and the car leaps forward.

The cars speeding along the streets are of many different colors, cherry red, light blue, yellow, and black. This means chemical plants have made paints of different colors.

The headlights of the cars glow, and the windows flash sunshine in our eyes. This means that glass factories have made glass and an electric light bulb factory has made headlights for the cars.

There are tyres. So a tyre factory must have done some work.

On the seats there is a shaggy material, the work of textile mills.

Music plays softly inside the cars. A radio factory must have assembled radios for them.

And the engines came from a factory that makes car engines.

Once I tried to count how many factories help to make a car, and I lost count. There are hundreds of them, too many to count. Yet we say, "A car is made in a car factory." That is true. A big car factory turns out a car

every minute. Just imagine! A car a minute! It takes more than a minute to read a page in a book. Just think how important it is to be careful about every minute in a car factory.

A car a minute!

A car a minute!

At all the plants and factories that make textiles, tyres, glass and everything else people have to be careful about Time, because these minutes connect all of them with the car factory. Time unites working people.

A car a minute!

A car a minute!

ROLLING MILL
GLASS FACTORY
CHEMICAL PLANT
TEXTILE MILL
fender
tyre
cable
glass windows
petrol
paints
lamps
seats

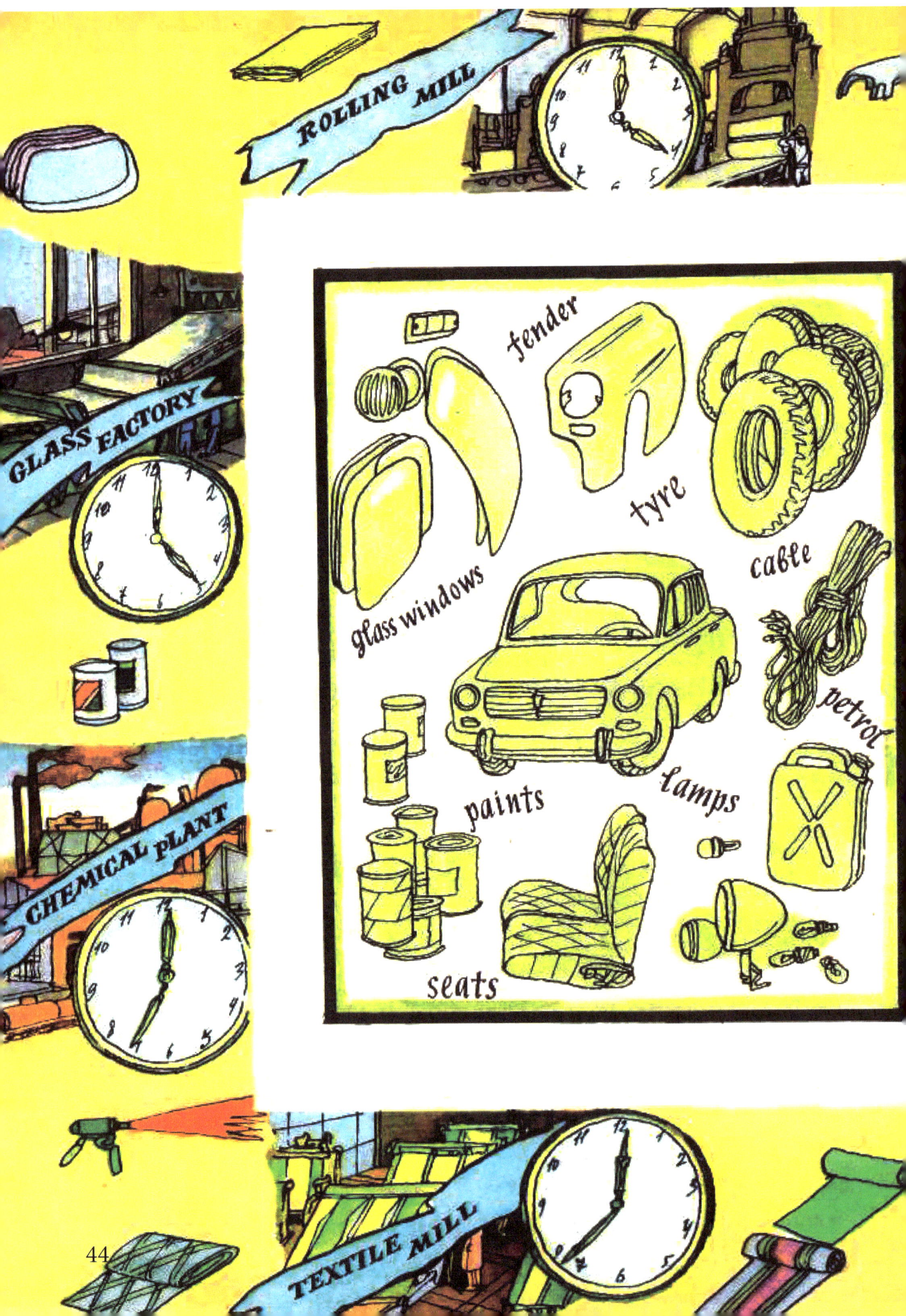

44

If there is a holdup anywhere, if just one of the factories works slowly, do you know what will happen? The main factory, the car factory, may stop working.

For this reason all the factories and plants have one common and strict PLAN.

The Plan says what each must do.

It states how many cars and parts to make and how much cloth to weave.

It states how quickly the factories and plants must get all the work done, by what day they must finish.

Headlights, red rear lights and tyres must all reach the car factory exactly on Time. The schedule is exact. The plan is exact, so that the workers at the car factory can also work exactly according to plan. After all, if they hurry, they may not tighten the screws enough, they may not adjust the engine exactly right. You know the saying "Haste makes waste." Otherwise, a car will be nice to look at but will not run as it should. It will be of poor quality. When workers work according to plan and watch the hours and minutes, they make cars that will serve people for a long time without breaking down, that is, cars of excellent quality.

All machinery and instruments must be made well. Quality is as valuable as every minute of working time.

What is a minute worth?

It is worth more than gold. Every minute the coal mines of the Soviet Union produce thirty freight cars of coal, the oil fields produce enough oil to fill twenty tank cars, and enough steel comes out of the burning hot furnaces to make thirty motor cars. Just think! All in the same minute!

And in that same minute... No, it is impossible to list

everything. Our factories and plants are giants. So every minute is precious.

While reading this book, you have grown half an hour or a whole hour older. Time marches on.

Tomorrow will be tomorrow!

20
TANK CARS

ONE
MINUTE

300
MOTOR CA